About the Author

Born in 1979, Rania Mamoun is a Sudanese author, journalist and activist. She has published two novels in Arabic – *Green Flash* (2006) and *Son of the Sun* (2013) and her short stories have been published in various magazines and anthologies, including *The Book of Khartoum* (Comma Press, 2016), the first ever anthology of Sudanese short fiction in translation. She has also worked as a culture editor for *Al-Thaqafi* magazine, a columnist for *Ad-Adwaa* newspaper and presenter of the 'Silicon Valley' cultural programme on Sudanese TV. *Thirteen Months of Sunrise* is her debut collection.

Thirteen Months of Sunrise

RANIA MAMOUN

Translated by Elisabeth Jaquette

First published in Great Britain by Comma Press, 2019.
www.commapress.co.uk

First published in Arabic by Dar Azmina, 2009.

A CIP catalogue record of this book is available from the British Library.

ISBN-10 1910974390
ISBN-13 978-1-91097-439-1

This book has been selected to receive financial assistance from
English PEN's 'PEN Translates' programme. The book was also supported
by the PEN/Heim Translation Fund.

The publisher gratefully acknowledges the support of Arts Council England.

For my father Ali,
my brother Wada'a,
and my friend Ibtihal, with whom I postponed a phone call,
one I never made.

I love you.

Contents

Thirteen Months of Sunrise

THIRTEEN IS NOT A SUPERSTITIOUS or unlucky number, it's the number of months in a year in Ethiopia.

But that's another story.

I was very frustrated by the time he arrived. The computer in front of me had frozen and a customer needed help. It was morning and I was still half-asleep.

I assumed he was Sudanese when I saw him, or, more accurately, I didn't assume anything. It wouldn't have been unusual to meet a Sudanese man in my country. Isn't it normal for Sudanese people to live in Sudan? I don't know why I didn't ask myself where he was from when he spoke to me in English. Maybe my mind was elsewhere.

I fixed the problem with the computer and was in a better mood. I overheard him grumbling about a floppy disk.

'You're not worth the trouble', he muttered to it.

'You're better off using a CD or a flash drive,' I told him. 'They're safer. You really shouldn't trust floppy disks nowadays.'

'Yes, I won't again.'

'Do you have a copy of what was on the disk?'

'Yes, but just a print version. I'd hoped to edit it.'

'Eritrean or Ethiopian?' I asked.

'Ethiopian,' he said with pride.

Before we met, I hadn't really known the difference between Ethiopia and Eritrea. I didn't know why I preferred the idea of Eritrea and its capital, Asmara, to Ethiopia and Addis Ababa. Even though I'd never visited either country, I felt that Eritrean rhythms spoke to my soul somehow and the same with Asmara. I liked both countries, generally speaking, and had harboured a great love for Abyssinia ever since I was small. We lived next door to an 'Abyssinian' bookshop, a word we used to refer to all Ethiopian and Eritrean immigrants and visitors to Sudan.

The bookshop occupied the whole building and hosted community events and gatherings when I was young. In front of it was a vacant lot where teenagers played football. It was lined with houses that had little gardens in front, each ringed with barbed wire, wooden posts, or mats. They often held celebrations in that open area by erecting a stage, setting out lots of chairs, and pitching a large tent over the top.

I loved how the Abysinnians danced, the intense way they moved their shoulders and neck with the beat. I still do. I often stared at the dancers on stage, gazing at the women's beautiful clothes, white with colourful embroidery, with my hands full of popcorn and mouth agape.

We didn't understand anything they were saying or singing because they spoke and sang in Amharic, but even so, we delighted in the melodies, music, dancing, and joyous atmosphere.

The Abyssinians were a vital part of the community with their gatherings, just like the other adults and children in the neighbourhood. We shared their delight in the festivities. For us, the parties were a chance to play and cause mischief; we'd stand on either side of the tent, batting at each other through the fabric. Anyone who wanted a seat had to fight for it, there was always chaos, commotion, and clamour. It was our chance to escape the adults' supervision and revel in childhood freedom.

'I really love Abyssinia,' I told him.

'We look the same, so we feel an affinity with each other. You're wearing clothing similar to ours, by the way.'

I was wearing an abaya and matching trousers made from handwoven fabric on the loom. It was white with brown threads running through it, and three red stripes embroidered on the cuff... it really did look like Abyssinian attire. In fact, I remember asking the tailor who made it to use red because it made the outfit look more Abyssinian.

Perhaps the abaya I was wearing reminded him of home, perhaps that's what drew him to me. When you're homesick, you yearn for anything familiar: people, language, signs, anything. We feel differently towards these things than we do when we're nestled in our own country's embrace.

A beautiful friendship took seed in those moments. He told me it pained him that he couldn't easily communicate with other people, not without constantly explaining and clarifying, but with the two of us, conversation was easy. He found in me someone who understood him, and I found in him a window into Ethiopia, and oh how I loved it.

He mispronounced my name for the first few days, calling me 'Raina' instead of 'Rania,' half-swallowing the 'R', while I called him 'Kidane'.

Back home, Kidane is a woman's name, he told me, 'Call me Kidana.'

'For us, Kidana is a woman's name,' I told him, 'because it ends in an "a".'

I would ask him about all sorts of things, from *zaghny* (an Ethiopian dish) and *zaleekh* (chilli), to politics and Eritrea's conflicts with Ethiopia, born from Italian colonialism. He told me how, when Eritreans wanted their own currency in place of the Ethiopian *birr*, their former Prime Minister, Meles Zenawi, deceived them by just changing the design.

He compared everything, great and small, to what it was like in his country, and he often said that he never imagined that he might sit, chat, laugh, and enjoy a beautiful friendship with a Sudanese woman. We joked and drank tea, 7Up, and tamarind juice, which he said, with its brown colour, looked like an alcoholic drink they have back home.

He asked me to accompany him to buy some Sudanese music, so we went to Studio Adeel and Zein. I picked out a cassette tape featuring some of the greatest Sudanese singers for him, as well as one of the flautist Hafiz Abdelrahman called *Everlasting Days*.

'Think of me every time you listen to those tapes,' I told him.

'I'll fall in love with you if I do that.'

'No. You mustn't fall in love with me.'

'I love you now, in my own way.'

'I love you, too, in my own way.'

Little Mohamed, who was twelve years old and worked at the café on weekends, always stared curiously at us when we were together, trying to get closer to us.

'He's Sudanese?' he asked me one day.

'Kind of,' I replied.

'Then why doesn't he speak Arabic... was he in America or something?'

I laughed and told Kidane what the boy said. Kidane laughed too.

'He's Ethiopian,' I said.

'Y'mean Abyssinian.'

'Yes, Abyssinian.'

'So you're Abyssinian, too,' he said to me.

I laughed again.

'My mother is Abyssinian.'

'Is that guy related to you?'

'Yes, he's my cousin.'

After that Mohamed began to show off his knowledge of English, which didn't seem to include more than ten words. Kidane became far more relaxed around him, and from then on they were friends.

I wouldn't claim I could speak English like a 'Johnny,' as we called the English, but through it we were able to understand each other.

Kidane was able to communicate with the words he knew, as well as a generous human spirit. I didn't need him to finish every sentence he began, and if I got a word wrong he never corrected or embarrassed me.

Kidane was here to collect data on water for his Master's thesis. He was researching the Nile basin and had been given a choice: travel to Sudan or Egypt. He chose the former. He was here to study the Gezira Scheme – the largest irrigation project on the continent of Africa – and was doing fieldwork at the scheme's headquarters in Barakat, with farmers in the villages of Helwa and Bika, in the city of al-Hasaheisa, and at the Agricultural Research Authority in Wad Madani.

'We drink the same water,' he said to me once.

'Yes,' I replied. 'It flows through both of us.'

The Blue Nile, which passes through Khartoum, originates at Lake Tana in Ethiopia. That's what makes our bond so strong, I thought: we were nursed from the same source. The White Nile originates at Lake Victoria in Uganda and the two rivers – the unruly Blue Nile, and the wide, calm White Nile – meet in Khartoum, where their beauty glorifies the city. There they converge to form the great River Nile, which crosses Egypt to where it then flows into the Mediterranean Sea.

It's 'tea' in Amharic, and 'teha' in Tigrinya, he told me every time I ordered a cup of tea. He knew both languages: Amharic, which was spoken by the Amhara people, and Tigrinya, which was spoken by the Tigrayans. His father was Tigrayan and his mother was Amhara. He told me about the different tribes and ethnicities back home: Muslims from Harar, beautiful men and women who still live in cities surrounded by huge walls like ancient citadels; the Afar people, the Oromo, Somalis and those from the South, and the Anuak people, who intersected with part of the Dinka tribe in South Sudan.

When I was little, a friend told me that she had a relative from Ethiopia, and he'd told her that their year had thirteen months.

This tale stayed in the back of my mind, and once, when we were browsing an Ethiopian website, I asked him, what's the story?

'Each of our months has just thirty days, and all the extra days from months which have thirty-one days are combined to make the thirteenth month of the year,' he told me. '*Pagumen* is the name of the thirteenth month, which has five or six days depending on whether it's a leap year.' How could Pagumen be a month when it had fewer days than a week? Ethiopia was a wonderous country!

It's the only nation in the world with a year unlike all the others – a year with an extra month, a composition all its own – and whenever I recalled this, I would ask the person next to me: did you know that Ethiopia has thirteen months?

'Is this place good for you?' He asked as we were deciding where to sit.

'It's not the place that's important, but the person you share it with. They can make it heaven or hell.'

'In that case it's definitely good for you!'

We laughed a lot that day, and when he said, 'I feel at home in this country,' I was filled with joy that I'd managed to ease his sharp loneliness. When he walked away, on that last day together, I felt as if a strong hand had clasped my heart and squeezed it tight, and I couldn't look away until he'd disappeared from sight.

It was evening, and in front of us was a wide, green field ringed by young trees. 'Open spaces nourish the imagination,' said my Ethiopian friend. Did I imagine something different about him that last evening? He was different, yes. Or at least that's how I felt, because my feelings for him were different, feelings preceding the word goodbye. Maybe for forever. In my mind, I told him: take care of yourself... keep in touch... please, don't forget what we shared.

I felt the moment of farewell sweep over me, and the consequences that usually accompany those moments.

'Will I see him again someday, somewhere?' I asked someone nearby.

Kidane Kiros was his name.

Passing

HE VISITS ME OFTEN, asking the same question in the same tone of sorrow.

'Why don't you become a doctor like you promised me?'

'I'm not going to, I'm sorry,' I tell him with regret.

'I put my hopes in you, and thought you would make them come true,' he says.

I fall silent, unable to respond. Or perhaps it's the disappointment flowing through his words that leaves me mute.

The cracks in the walls are stained with the scent of you, mixed with particles of dust. It seeps into me, the air in the room is flooded with it. I look around, trying to find the source. It fills me, engulfs me. I stretch out my hand to take it in my palm, for it to touch me, for me to touch you through it, to touch your tender palm, your face, your hand. I feel you close to me… so close. I feel you near me, within me, inside of me. If I reach out, I think, I might collide with you.

Your scent opens channels of memory, it invades me without warning, like armies of ants stinging me fiercely, chaotically: on my eyes, my skin, in my pores, my blood, even my ears, as they pick up the vibrations of your voice drawing closer. I'm flooded with memories: I feel the warmth of your embrace; the warmth of the bed where as a child I slept beside you instead of Mother; you coming home from your errands, me sticking to you like glue. Mother tried to separate me from you, but I didn't listen. 'He's going on a trip tomorrow,' she'd tell me, and I'd say: 'But he'll come back.'

Now that I'm grown, that you have left, that I have surrendered to a loss so hard to abide, I can't give the same answer, or even be so sure.

Your scent fills every inch of space. It pulls me out of a whirlpool of memory, tosses me into another, wider and deeper, and the feeling that you are close to me swells. You sip your tea from the big mug we kept – how you loved your tea – and then listen to the radio, lying on your back with one leg crossed over the other. You rifle through your satchel of memories, and call me over to read one. Sometimes your shadow deceives me, as you wash before prayer. I remember how happy you were when we moved to the house next to the mosque, where the call to prayer was so loud it beat in our hearts and shook our bodies, and you said, 'Nothing makes me happier than being near the mosque, could we wish for a better neighbour?'

Today is the Eid. Everyone flits around joyously. From the mosque, the muezzin calls out:

Allahuakbar. Allahuakbar. La ilahailla Allah. Allahuakbar we lillah al-hamd.

God is great. God is great. There is no god but God. God is great, praise God.

And the children repeat it after him. My nieces and nephews race in and out, delighted with their new clothes, Eid sweets never leaving their mouths. They rush up to me, all abuzz.

'Where are our Eid presents?' asks Eyad. 'And don't say you'll hand them out later!'

'We want them now, we're going to the swings,' says Bara'a.

'How much'll you give us?' asks Ziad. 'We always get lots for Eid. Please, we want lots of coins.'

I'm nearly done tidying the house. I straighten the carpets, pull fresh sheets taut on the beds, and add more embers to the incense burner. The scent of sandalwood wafts up, crowning the festivities.

I hear my sister calling out to Mother.

'Mum… Mum… come look at Dad. What's wrong with him? He doesn't look well at all.'

Mother comes. She feels his forehead. She asks him something, he doesn't respond. She tells my sister to call our neighbour, the doctor.

My sister has already bathed him today, dressed him in a new *jellabiya*, and daubed on his cologne. She tells him today is Eid, but he doesn't seem to understand what she's saying or even know what day it is. He's completely out of it. You ask him something and he doesn't respond, or even give the impression he hears you. When he looks at you, you can't tell whether he sees you, or if he's looking right through you. His eyes wander, lost in empty space.

She brings him his favourite tea, takes him back to bed, and tucks him in.

'Did he drink the tea?' I ask her. 'Did he throw it up?'

'Yes, he drank it. But I don't know whether he'll keep it down or not.'

I was his favourite child, he loved me so much. Whenever he saw me sitting quietly by myself, not chatting with the rest of the family late into the evening, he would come up to me and ask, 'What's the matter? Why are you sitting here alone?'

'Nothing's the matter… I'm just sitting here.'

'Go on, go sit and chat with your siblings, I don't like to see you sitting by yourself like this.'

He brought treats just for me: candy, spare change, sugar cane juice, peanuts, snacks. He showered me with affection, sat me next to him, everything, and when my siblings protested, he told them I was the 'last grape in the bunch', the baby of the family.

When I came home from school and asked Mother about lunch, he was the one who would tell me, 'Go to the kitchen, don't be shy. It's your house, go get yourself something to eat.'

He announced his highest hopes for me – this daughter of mine, I want her to be a doctor. He called me *Miss Doctor* and I loved it. But after all his tenderness, I couldn't give him what he wanted.

Waiting for the doctor, I sit by his head as he lies on the bed. I notice droplets of sweat on his brow and bald head. I wipe them away with my hand, without a tissue. His forehead grows damp again, I wipe it again. It keeps growing damp, and I keep wiping it with my bare hand.

When the doctor arrives he finds us gathered around him, Mother rubbing his feet as they spasm, my sister on the other side of the bed holding his hand, my brother standing nearby, and me by his head, wiping his forehead again and again. The doctor examines him closely. Mother follows Father's gaze. Maybe she realises what's happening. She begins to repeat the *shahada* and the doctor does not ask her to be quiet. He takes Father's blood pressure and opens his eyes and takes his pulse. I see my father's eyelids flutter, and he repeats the *shahada* after my mother, in a voice so low it can barely be heard. Then his voice fades and his eyelids' fluttering slows.

In a decisive moment, his forehead is drenched in sweat. His lips stop moving and the doctor looks up with regret.

In my ignorance, I didn't realise until right then that I was wiping traces of sweat from the spirit's parting; I didn't even know it was gone. Perhaps it passed right next to me. Perhaps it brushed against me as it left. Perhaps it bade me farewell, waved or smiled, but even though I was so close, I did not see it at all.

Edges

I HAD WAITED FOR HIM for so many years. For him to come mend my cracks and fissures.

He came to dismantle, disperse, and then assemble me, to rearrange my parts and pieces, to shape me anew. He came to make the desires I hid from even my friends come true: *I wanted a love that would rip through me like a spear.*

'Have you really been ripped through by a spear? Has it moved you so much, and brought you enough pain to fill your writing?'

'I write to recount my tragedies.'

'No, you write to keep them inside you, and give them new life with each story.'

'Maybe… shouldn't you leave and let me finish this?'

'You know I can't leave you.'

'Then quiet down and forget about my writing. I'm almost done.'

'I see you've changed the beginning. I don't like seeing her with a spirit so crushed, so defeated.'

'Is that how you read it? Well, I'll change it, just promise you won't keep interrupting me.'

'I can't do that.'

'Try.'

Our relationship is strange, surprising, crazy, untameable, fierce. No words can describe it: it rebels against language, snubs and ignores it. It's the kind of thing you feel but cannot describe. A thrumming deep in my veins, which seeps out between words and the pauses between them, like plumes of smoke so hard to grasp. Trying to pin it down is a waste of time and energy, any attempt makes you lose the feeling, the moment.

She's always here, close to me. Sometimes I get annoyed by how she forces herself into my most hidden corners. I pick fights with her, I get angry, I gather my secrets and toss them beyond consciousness. I hide them seven earths deep inside me and then rejoice, thinking that I've set her on the wrong path, that she'll lose her way, only to realise that the one who is lost is me.

She's a good reader; she can read me no matter how poor my handwriting, no matter how vague my words. She enters me through my eyes, staring into them for so long that it begins to hurt. 'The eyes are the window to the soul,' she often says, and is really convinced of that.

As soon as he arrived, I loved him like I shouldn't have; so much I felt like I could hardly breathe. It suffused me.

'That was your mistake,' she said to me.

'Was it wrong of me to love someone?'

'What was wrong was loving the wrong person.'

She always seems to know so much, to know everything about me, the minutia of my daily life, the depths of my interior, how my nails grow inconsolably long, and my feet are cracked and dirty. She knows about the little razor cut on my left index finger from sharpening a pencil, and my ill will towards my neighbour. She knows everything *about me*. *That's why* I trusted her, and why I changed my story: because she didn't like the beginning. Or rather, because *it* didn't please *her*.

She partakes in every word I write, every idea I pursue and every train of thought I follow. She reads all of my words, and also what's hidden in them. Sometimes it's buried in my subconscious and she extracts it, explains it, cleans it, shines it, then shows it to me.

When I first started seeing him, we often disagreed. She wanted me to be sensible and love him bit by bit, and I refused.

'You mean I should love him in installments?' I asked sarcastically.

'Fine. Have it your way,' she replied angrily. 'But remember, I see things you don't.'

We argued and then she disappeared for a time, and all the while I could feel birds of paradise fluttering in my heart.

'Remember?'

I remember the evening the damp sandbar lay between us and the Blue Nile, when he reached out and said, 'Give me your hand.'

I lived a lifetime in the space and time between when I lifted my hand – it moved through the air, reached its apex, began its descent – and when it settled in his palm. I experienced a whole lifetime, parallel to my own, in those moments.

When the current took hold of me completely, I felt it in my very core, with every atom of my being. It was so clear, powerful, and moving, that just thinking of him brought me back to that moment, with its potent energy and emotion.

That evening I went to her, called out to her, made amends with her. I confessed to her that I wasn't happy – I was happiness itself.

Out of kindness of heart, she didn't spoil my moment. She shared it with me, and we celebrated together; we danced, sang, called out, and slept deeply. She wasn't cross with me afterwards, but she still treated my nascent love with clear caution and apprehension.

I was consumed by love's sweetness, freshness and tenderness. Even so, I missed her immensely when she was gone. At night I would think of my lover, but wind up thinking of her. Instead of dreaming of him, she was the one who came to me.

She visited me at work too. Whenever I focused on something other than her, she always became resentful and accused me of ignoring her, so I would put everything else aside.

She chose specific times for us to go to the cafeteria together, for a cup of tea or coffee or whatever we were in the mood for. The cafeteria workers stared at me quizzically; which I figured, at the time, was because we were the only two people in the cafeteria instead of the office. She'd stay with me until the end of my shift, and then we'd buy nuts and cross the road to the bus together, chatting and laughing, having fun cracking the shells in the street, so different from the stillness of eating them at home.

She came up with an idea that day: we should walk every street in the city, indulging our love for long walks. I hesitated.

'That's crazy, let's take a taxi,' I said.

'If we do that, we'll never have walked every inch of the city we love. So what if we get tired and our feet swell? We'll soak them in salt water. We'll have spent hours and hours walking, and will have proved our love for this city, that we belong to it and appreciate all of it.'

'Prove our love with how tired we are?'

'No, with our knowledge… in knowing that our dear city is filled with love.'

We walked and walked for three days. We walked without sleep or food, from neighbourhood to neighbourhood, alleyway to alleyway, street to street. For a week after that I didn't leave the house, I couldn't place my feet on the ground. She would visit me and laugh.

'See how fragile you are?' she said.

The words rang in my ears for a long time. The weight of her words landed in that barren space within me and took root. Yes, I had become fragile. After I lost him, anything could break me. There was a vast emptiness inside me waiting for him. I'd become as hollow as a reed, or flute, unable to hold a note.

If a pin dropped on the ground, the whole universe and everything inside it would be able to hear the echo. It's so cruel to live life alongside a void.

'That last sentence isn't accurate.'

'What is it with you, sticking your nose in, between my pen and paper? What I wrote is precisely how I feel.'

'Yes I know, but where am I in all of this? You should say, "It's so cruel to live life alongside a void, *and her.*"'

I laughed.

'But life isn't cruel when we're together,' I told her. 'I don't even know how I'd get by without you. What good would it do to imagine that?'

'We have on this earth what makes life worth living, as Darwish said.' A tearful smile appeared on her face. 'What good am I if you miss him so much, if it hurts this bad? I should leave you.'

'You know I can't survive without you. You're like a cloud, bringing rain to the parched earth.'

In one of her strange attempts to be certain of our love for each other, we spent seventy-five hours without leaving one another's side, not even for a moment. We didn't sleep, or read, or write, or eat. Nothing. We were simply together, in the truest sense of the word.

At the time, I didn't try to contradict her or disagree with her or rationalise her strange and wild tendencies. I gave myself to her completely, and she led me to places of happiness that I had never known. She took me to heavenly places where people were dressed in white and green, and were floating above the ground as if swimming in air. Their hands fluttered like wings, their faces were smiling, content and happy. The sight of them was magnificent to behold, and it delighted her.

'Are those angels?' I asked her, astonished.

She smiled and shook her head.

'They're people just like you, only they're happy.'

She took me to places where the air was pure and the fields were verdant green; places with flowing rivers, where the mountains and clouds shielded your skin from the sun.

'This is our secret, don't write about it.'

'Why not?'

'They'll think it exists in your mind.'

'It doesn't matter what they think. They don't matter to me anymore, not my family, nor my neighbours. Not even the cafeteria staff.'

She looked at me for a long time, perhaps trying to decide how much she believed me despite what she knew. Or maybe she wanted to enjoy what I'd said. Then she smiled, and I glimpsed contentment on her face.

She hugged me gleefully.

'You're my soul,' she told me.

'You're my angel.'

'I'll let you finish your writing without interruption.'

'Good. You look tired. Perhaps you should get some rest.'

'I really am tired,' she said. 'I'll lay down next to you.'

Within a few moments, she was fast asleep.

I studied her closely. It was the first time she had gone to bed before me, and the first time I was truly seeing her. Usually I looked at her the way people look at everyone who has gone through difficult times with them: quickly, without thought, barely registering them. But this moment offered itself up to real sight.

Beautiful, faithful, loving and beloved. I saw her before me in flesh and blood. I touched her. Everyone said she lived in my mind alone, some of them swore I was living in a fantasy, others thought I was imagining things, and others accused me of being crazy.

I don't know how I found her, or when. I didn't know anything about her. I wasn't sure of anything any more.

I don't know if our relationship had a starting point. Perhaps she had been born alongside me, an invisible twin. Or perhaps she emerged from me at a time I can't recall. Perhaps she *was* me. Or perhaps it was like she said: that she was born from a story. If that was the case, I still don't know if she emerged from someone else's story or one of my own.

I had no interest in finding out or knowing for sure, her presence itself was enough for me. Beginnings and endings didn't really matter, nor did learning the real answer.

They say I can no longer distinguish between reality and fantasy, a polite way of saying that I'm delusional. They take me to doctors and sheikhs and therapists, they make me take medicine and waft smoke over me from the sheikh's incense papers.

They insist they don't see her, but I see her as vividly as I see them. I see her sharing my solitude, making me laugh, quarrelling with me, interrupting my train of thought, messing up my writing. She's there in every moment, helping me overcome my disappointments in love, commiserating with me over my losses and sharing her strange, crazy self.

Who's right, them or me?

I'd never wondered whether she was really there, despite everyone around me saying she wasn't real.

To me, she seems quite normal. She eats like me, sleeps like me, laughs like me, walks on the ground like me. But she doesn't cry like me, she's the one who wipes away my tears. Is that why they want her to leave? Don't they know my life is bound to her, that we cannot be separated?

She turns over onto her left side and has her back to me now. The blanket slips off, and I draw it back over her. I kiss her forehead. My eyes don't leave her. I smile because she makes me so happy, because of how much I love her. My partner, my other self, the sweetest hour of my days.

In her untroubled sleep, I find an opportunity to write without interruption about all the things spinning inside of me. I organise my papers, pour myself a cup of tea, turn the page, and begin writing anew.

A Week of Love

Day One

WE MET UP AS PEOPLE DO. He didn't make an impression.

Day Two

We sat side by side, he edged closer. I felt his gaze engulf me. I smiled to myself. He had beautiful eyes.

Day Three

He asked me whether I was seeing anyone.

I responded with silence. Maybe silence was malice on my part.

Day Four

He told me: 'I love you, I've never had feelings like this before.' And I felt myself falling for him; in my heart I accepted his love.

Day Five

When I arrived he was waiting for me. He was early. I'd grown used to him.

Day Six

I felt my ribcage expand with him. He was late, he hadn't arrived yet even though he'd promised. I waited, and waited, and waited even longer, but he didn't show up. My temperature climbed higher. I called him and when he picked up his voice sounded cold, vacant, dead.

Day Seven

I texted him: 'This is hard for me. Going back is hard. Going forward is hard. And standing here is torture. Please, be a friend to me.'

In the Muck of the Soul

Wide shot

A WOMAN BENDS DOWN to pick up a stone and launches it towards the dogs barking at her. The hour is past midnight. Huge pickups and freight trucks pass her as she walks along the uneven ground that rises and falls. Behind her is a pack of dogs, and the darkness that makes it even harder to go on.

Ruff ruff ruff.

Grrrrgrrrr.

She continues throwing stones until she runs out, and then bends down to pick up more.

Grrrgrrrgrrrr.

She tries to reach the pavement where there is more light, maybe just enough to see with.

A military patrol drives the dogs away with a gunshot, which plunges through the calm and quiet night, sending ripples across its surface.

Two shot

A deep brusque voice:

'Where you walking to tonight, ma'am? What kind of person goes out at this hour?'

'Would I have left home if I didn't have good reason? I'm going to Khartoum.'

'That's not safe for you. What's waiting for you in Khartoum?'

'There's… never mind.'

Flashback

The woman moves restlessly through a cramped room, looking for something to ease his pain; she picks up a packet of pills, sees that it's empty, throws it away, notices a bottle of medication, prays to God, tosses it aside, rummages in a bag on the desk near the bed; the bag is filled with prescriptions, flyers for medications, used syringes and empty blister packs.

She looks at him, still squirming in pain, and helps him to sit up. His scream fills her head; she runs outside and stops in the narrow courtyard lined with straw, where some of the green clay walls are still unfinished.

She goes back inside and asks herself: *what can I do?*

She sees that he's given up on the bed and thrown himself on the floor; she tries to lift him up and can't, tries again and still can't. She cries and runs outside again, goes to the clay urn, pours him some water, asks him to drink a cup to ease his pain, but he refuses. She begs, he takes a sip and looks at her, he's silent and feels bad, then steels himself, and with her help, lifts himself back into bed to let the torture begin all over again.

Night shot

    'Where are you going, ma'am?'

    'I…'

    'It looks to me like you might need a ride.'

    'Thank you… I can't tell you what a help that would be.'

Long shot

Men huddle on the pavement in front of the charity office. Some have wrapped themselves in blankets, turbans and rags, and are lying down. Others are sitting, discussing their woes. A few are nervous and remain standing, moving around, coming and going, maybe trying to keep warm.

Medium shot

Two women with an infant spread out several pieces of cardboard along an open-air corridor, and lay down opposite a little wooden service window that is closed. They are bundled up, and one young woman tries to use a piece of cardboard to cover her bare feet.

    'Good evening.'

    'Good evening to you,' responds the young woman. The older woman rubs her forehead, rearranges her things, and goes back to sleep.

    'I thought I'd be the first one here!'

    'We've been here since ten this morning,' the young

woman says, and hands her a piece of paper. 'You'll need to fill out your name, here,' she adds.

'I don't know how to write… can you write it for me?'

'You're number fifteen.'

'When did the others sign up?'

'Some folks write their names and leave, and then come back early in the morning. But it's best if you're sitting here when they call you.'

For a moment the woman stands there in silence. There's a large rock nearby, and she thinks about sitting against it, until she hears the young woman speak to her again.

'Go over to that officer there, and he'll give you some cardboard to spread out like this. He's the one who gave this to us.'

The woman goes to get some cardboard, she has no other choice. She can't sit on the rock until morning; she has cystitis, and the cardboard will be more comfortable.

Flashback

'One kidney has permanently failed, and the other is on its way. He needs a transplant.'

'You mean there's no cure?'

'There is a cure – he needs a new kidney.'

'This operation, how much does it cost?'

'A lot.'

45-degree angled shot

A hospital bed. The woman sits next to it, nearby is a desk.

A faint voice: 'Mum, let me die.'

'And what'll happen to me, then?'

'The operation's expensive. Where will we get that kind of money?'

'God is generous, my son, he'll provide for us.'

Dialogue

'Do the operation, out of the goodness of your heart, and I'll pay you when he recovers.'

'An operation out of the goodness of my heart, ma'am? The hospital runs on money not goodwill.'

'You mean you're going to let him die?' Her accusation steals his breath.

'I have a solution for you, but there's no guarantee. Write to the charity office and ask them to cover part of the cost.'

'And the rest of it?'

'I'll pay for it. May God grant you easier times.'

'Thank God for you, Doctor. God bless you.'

A smile spreads across her face.

Medium shot

An office with three desks. A man rests his feet on a desk, solving a crossword, with a half-empty cup of tea beside him.

Outside, the woman knocks on the door, receives no response, knocks again, and begins to doubt whether anyone is there. She peers inside, glimpses a shoe, cranes her neck to see more, and spots the employee.

Camera tracks the woman's movement

She steps inside and greets him, still to no response. He seems irritated to see her. She gives up on hoping he'll respond with a hello… and starts explaining what she needs.

'I have the papers for my sick son.'

'What's he got?' He says without raising his head from the newspaper.

'It's his kidneys.'

'We only take serious diseases like that two days a week, Saturday and Wednesday. Get here early 'cause it's always busy, and make sure you bring all the paperwork.'

Medium shot

Same location as before. Open-air corridor in front of the wooden service window, thirty women sit on dirt and cardboard, two sharing the rock. Time: 4:30am.

The woman listens to the others nearby.

'When will the window open?'

'In half an hour.'

'We'll meet the committee exhausted like this?'

'Of course. They might give you money or they might not.'

'How many people does the committee see?'

'Fifty, but that's both men and women.'

'I've come three times now, and every time they only let in a certain number of people. I told myself this time I have to spend the night.'

'I've been coming for three months; every Saturday

and Wednesday I'm here, and every time they tell me some form is missing; every time I bring them new forms they tell me another one's missing.'

'This is the first time I've been here,' says another woman. 'We sold the house for Mother's treatment, but the money still wasn't enough, so we were forced to come here. Me and my brothers decided that charity was our only hope.'

'The money they give out isn't enough, but it's better than nothing.'

Close-up

The woman's face: slender, brown, exhausted, sad. Wrinkles have settled on her face, especially around her mouth and eyes. Hollow eyes, somewhat prominent cheeks. Under her headscarf, wisps of white carve through the black. Her gaze is steady, but her mind wanders.

'I don't have a house to sell, or brothers to make the decision with… It's just me and him,' she says to no one in particular.

The shot zooms in, focuses on her eyes, luminous eyes filled with pain, fixed on a point in the distance. After an age she blinks, a sign that the scene in her mind has changed.

Tears tumble from her eyes. The camera pans down to a fallen tear, the focus sharpens and it fills the screen.

The tear is a great, transparent orb of water, an ocean in which her late husband appears, lying on a low, woven cot, an *anqareeb*. In real time, their son, a boy once more, plays with his father's moustache, plucking at it and then jumping about rambunctiously, and she sits there laughing happily, beside three cups and a pot of tea with milk.

Cut

Doors

HE WOKE UP EARLY, unusual for him, and got out of bed with cheerful enthusiasm.

He headed to the tap to wash his face and freshen his breath with minty toothpaste but discovered the water had been shut off. *God! When had they come? Did they never sleep!*

Then he remembered that he hadn't paid the utility bill this month. But how could he, if paying for water meant not paying for something else?

He could do without electricity for a month, without water for a month, without a phone for a month. He could stand the shopkeeper's frustrations and the landlord's provocations, and he swore, if the government allowed people to sleep on the streets, he could do without a house for a month, too. With that, he put 'house' on his 'marginal list', the list of things he could do without.

He tried not to give this trivial, inconsequential thing the pleasure of spoiling his good mood; he overcame it. He and his family always kept extra water just in case, and when that ran out, probably about two days into the shutoff, he could run a hose from his neighbour's house.

'Fill up a bucket and fast,' he shouted to his son. 'I need to shower and get out of here.'

He shut the bathroom door behind him, even though it was ridden with holes.

Cold water cascaded over his body and he felt invigorated. He wished the day would skip over the next two hours, cast them aside or return to them later. Either would be fine; what he wanted was to shut his eyes, open them, and find that it was nine o'clock, time to start his new job.

From that day forward he wouldn't have to wait for his brothers to send money sporadically from abroad; he wouldn't change his route to avoid the shopkeeper, or the butcher, or the neighbour who lent them part of his pension.

Their meals wouldn't follow the rule of 'here one day, gone the next, the third day only crumbs'; his children wouldn't go to bed without dinner, without even a little glass of milk.

'No no no… get out of here, boy… Mohammed, c'mere c'mere, your brother shoved the door. Ali grab that boy there, the door'll fall on his foot…'

The bathroom door was nothing more than a sheet of zinc with partially patched holes, but it mostly concealed whoever was behind it.

He got dressed without rinsing all the soap off his body, and swore that he would replace this corroded piece of zinc they generously called a door.

He made some tea, adding just a small pinch of sugar as usual. He put his faith in God, praised His name, and went to leave, but…

The front door! What was with the door? He tried to open it, pushed harder and harder, but it wouldn't budge. It was a double door, and one side was shorter than the other.

'Damn this warped door!' he said scornfully. 'Mohammed, I've told you a hundred times not to shut this *blasted door so hard… when you slam it, it sticks like this.*'

After a torrent of angry words he finally managed to open the door, with a screech heard by half of the neighbourhood. He looked down, and saw that the right sleeve of his freshly pressed shirt was now completely wrinkled.

But… no matter. He didn't want anything to spoil his mood. He tried to smooth the fabric with his other hand and kept walking. A bus was waiting and he quickly stepped aboard; he didn't want to be late for his first day.

'Get everyone in the doorway to move back into the bus, boy,' shouted the driver. 'Good lord, getting fined is the last thing we need this morning.'

As soon as the driver stopped speaking, the man felt himself being pushed by many hands and a struggle began.

'Brothers, please, move all the way in, God bless…'

One man punched his neighbour, the person next to him stamped on another one's foot, and a tall man was hunkered down so much it looked as if he were praying.

'Guys, open the window… it's hot, and meningitis is going around!' someone yelled.

Finally the bus arrived at the station. He pried himself from the crowd and sped off towards the office. Only when he arrived did he realise that the bus door had snagged his shirt. He tore off the flap of fabric and kept walking in his ripped shirt.

He went over it in his mind. *No one will notice the tear*, he convinced himself. He would try to stand so that no one could see it, and would buy a new shirt in a few days. He was a different man than he'd been yesterday when he was unemployed.

He entered the office owned by a certain businessman. (He was one of those men who appeared on the scene quite suddenly: rich, with an unknown past. All anyone knew was that he was a businessman. Since when, how? No one knew).

But… why should he care? It was none of his business, what mattered to him was this job, everything else was unimportant. He would work hard, prove his skills, and move up in life. Maybe this job would even open up other doors among the business elite.

The water would be turned back on, he wouldn't need to do without the things on his 'marginal list' – he'd have everything on the list every single month. He would buy a new bathroom door, install it himself, and repair the floor. He would fix the warped front door soon, too. They wouldn't need to skimp on sugar in their tea any more, even if it *was* healthier, and he would… he would… he would… He let himself sink into daydreams.

He reached the businessman's office on the second floor, and gazed at the beautiful door, solid and well-made. *It must be from a factory that makes doors and windows and other things, or maybe it's imported,* he thought to himself. At any rate, it definitely hadn't come from a workshop in the nearby industrial zone.

A sleek, elegant plaque was affixed up high, engraved with the word: *DIRECTOR*.

He felt the door, how cold it was, and took a deep breath. He grasped the handle and said to himself: *I've done it; at last I've made it into the world.*

But… What was wrong with it?! Why wouldn't it open? Was it warped like his front door? Or off its hinges like his bathroom door? Did it snatch clothing like the bus door?

He turned the handle a few times, knocked, knocked again, and then again, with no response.

An office boy passed by.

'Is the director in?' he asked the boy.

'You want the boss?'

'Of course I do, why else d'you think I asked?' he snapped.

'Are you Amr Ahmed?'

'Yes that's me, in flesh and blood.'

'Sorry, the boss said that when you arrived, to tell you that the position was offered to someone else, and he'd taken it.'

'What! What are you talking about?'

'Honest, that's what happened.'

Injustice… anger… rebellion. He banged on the

39

door and tried to force it open… and the hole in his shirt ripped further. What would happen to his children? He'd put all his hopes on this job, he deserved it, he was qualified, why had it been given to someone else? Why?!

He wouldn't leave without getting an answer to his questions, without knowing the reason. He thought about his situation, his house, his 'marginal list', his brothers who trickled support to him, his warped front door, the propped-up bathroom door.

Exhausted by everything he had been through, and desperately tired of thinking about tomorrow, he threw himself to the ground before the director's door and cried.

He cried feverishly, in defeat, out of a sense of injustice, and he lay there, intermittently lifting his gaze, wishing for it to open or for someone to look out. His wait stretched on, and the door stayed impassively shut.

A Woman Asleep
on Her Bundle

I DIDN'T THINK HER that tall or slender when I saw her sitting by the mosque wall. At night she was curled up, and in the morning she sat with her skinny legs outstretched.

I saw her carrying an old-fashioned bundle, oil-soaked and dark in hue, as she walked down the street, her legs long like crochet needles, taking lengthy strides. When you saw her, you forgot everything you knew about steady steps and straight lines. She seemed to have her own rhythm, her own sense of harmony: she leant to the right for a moment, then swerved to the left, in syncopated steps. She carried the bundle in her right hand and tucked the corner of her dress under her left arm, which swung freely by her side.

She took up residence by the mosque wall out of the blue, making a home under the neem trees with their dense foliage, trees whose leaves stand up straight and shade the area around them. There was lots of talk about her. Everyone had questions and everyone had answers, and while the answers differed, the stories all started the same way.

People who had lived in the neighbourhood for a long time said that she'd owned a house not far from the mosque, and that she'd once had money. But then 'Madame Cash' tricked her and took her house... although some people said she'd bought it. 'Madame Cash' earned her nickname because she had lots of money and gold, which her granddaughter once tried to steal to give to her father.

A lady whose name I don't know told me that the woman by the mosque had children, one of whom was a composer. When I asked why they let her live like this, she said the woman runs away from them: every time they take her back home, she refuses to stay.

I often saw her speaking to people that no one else could see, sometimes arguing with them or raising a threatening finger. On rare occasions she laughed and chatted amicably with them, but mostly she scolded them. Perhaps she contained too much anger, and that was the only way she could let it all out.

Many a time I tried to understand what she was saying by neatly sorting her words and storing them in my mind, but I never succeeded. From her expression and intonation, you could tell that she was speaking to an apparition, but you could never truly understand what she was saying. She had created her own world with them and immersed herself in it, unable to find her way out of their labyrinths, and uninterested in us curious passersby.

One of my sister's friends told me that children made fun of her, they cursed and threw stones at her because she often launched stones at people herself, and that one time she chucked rocks at a group of young girls just because they said hello. But since I'd never seen this myself, and since it seemed unlikely, I carried on greeting her every day, and she never threw a stone at me. Even so, that story stayed in the back of my mind, and every time I said good morning I imagined a rock flying at my head instead of a greeting in return.

One time I passed her, I noticed that she had long features, dark and deep-set eyes, face tattoos, and that her hair was thinning, perhaps with age.

She was always clean, never smelled bad and often glistened from the way she oiled her legs and hands. I often saw her moisturise, and sometimes I glimpsed her washing her clothes at the tap in the mosque before hanging them in some Good Samaritan's courtyard, either inside or in the open air. Opposite the mosque's eastern door, there was a walled-off area covered with hessian and plastic sheeting that was home to two scraggly neem trees that spread scant shade beneath them.

The woman changed her position as the sun moved. In the morning she sat on the north side of the wall, in the neem trees' shade, and in the afternoon she sat at the base of the wall on the east side, where shadows of trees and buildings advanced towards her. At night she sometimes curled up there, while other times she disappeared. Some people supposed that she slept in the mosque, while others guessed that she went to a courtyard across the street, to shelter from the rain like anyone else would. Either way, she always appeared shortly afterwards like a rainbow.

At night she laid her head on her dark bundle, and in the morning she always set it aside. The bundle intrigued me. She often gently rested a hand on it, or stroked it as tenderly as a mother running a hand through her child's hair, which always made me wonder. I asked myself: *Does it hold a precious treasure, her life's achievement? Or just a bunch of worthless odds and ends? Maybe it contains mementos from a past from which she alone survived?* She seemed like a deep well of secrets, and her bundle was a source of curiosity to me – every time my eyes fell on it, I felt compelled to find out more.

She unfurled a piece of hessian cloth to shield herself from the cold, while we considered if the thin dress she wore was enough cover. She kept a big tin can nearby which she drank from, a yellow plastic *kawra* that served as a bowl, a jar for her oils and old bottles of sparkling water, as well as other things I could never identify as I walked past.

I ran into my neighbour from across the street on the bus one day. She was carrying heavy bags laden with vegetables so I offered to walk her home. When we passed the woman, I gave her two tomatoes and a cucumber, and my neighbour said she would send her some bread.

'Why do her children let her live like this?' I asked, in yet another attempt to learn more about her. 'They shouldn't let her stray so far from home!'

'She's mad, and mad people don't let you tell them what to do,' my neighbour said.

'What's her story?' I asked.

'It's a long one. People say she went mad when she lost all her money. Lord protect us.'

'But she's not mad!' I said defensively.

'My dear, isn't it mad for someone to leave her home and go live in the street!'

This was her logic for convincing me that the woman was mad, but I refused to let it sway me. Nor would I believe that she was a beggar. She seemed self-aware to me, as if she'd chosen this life willingly for reasons that were hers alone. To me, she was unlike the crazy man who my friend Mohamed and I often saw on our way back from university. That man was very tall, and wore an old, discoloured jellabiya that stopped just above the knee. He looked, in other words, just like other crazy people who've decided to go about in rags. He used to wander down the middle of the street, walking on the asphalt as if it were a tightrope in the circus. He held his arms out to balance and took slow steps, incredibly carefully, perhaps thinking that the cars' blaring horns were the cheers of the crowd, and that the pedestrians were monkeys jumping about beneath him.

'He thinks the gravel is a rope!' I remember Mohamed saying.

'Samuel says that madness is an illusion,' I replied. 'He thinks he's tightrope walking. He believes his illusion, it's fixed in his mind.'

The woman with the bundle was also different to the man who walked through the market stark naked. Even when someone threw him a scrap of clothing he tore it up and stamped on it with his bare feet. It was a good thing I'd only seen him from behind and kept my distance. He'd once thrown something hard at my friend Souad and struck her on the head.

And she didn't beg like the woman who pan-handled on the unpaved road, or the one with elephantiasis outside the hospital, who asked me for more when I gave her 50 piasters, saying she'd pray hard for me. I gave her a pound, and she told me to give her the 50p too.

She was unlike all of them because she wasn't aggressive, quarrelsome, or sly. She didn't ask people for money, and yet, many passersby gave her what they could, as did the neighbours. One day as I was coming back from work I saw someone bring her a plate full of food, and collect another empty dish nearby. The woman thanked her and said a prayer for her, as she often said a prayer for me when I gave her a handful of change from my purse.

On one occasion she took a roll of blue paper from the pocket of her dress and showed it to me.

'Girl, will you tell me how much this is? Someone just gave it to me.'

'It's two of the new pounds, or two thousand pounds in the old piasters.'

'Huh! So he tricked me, gave me a useless scrap of paper.'

'No, Ma'am, they aren't useless… they're the new currency.'

I smiled as I walked away. I could tell that she understood. I was surprised by her scepticism – incredulity, perhaps – that someone would give her so much money.

Our eyes met and our fingers brushed against each other in that brief interaction. I touched her stiff, dry hand and half-expected it to crumble. I still wanted to sit with her every day, to have our morning coffee together and hear her stories, heedless of the dust kicked up by cars and inquiring looks from passersby.

I missed her when I didn't see her in her usual morning spot and I grew nervous, afraid I wouldn't find her there, or hear news of her departure. My heart felt ragged when I saw her at night at the base of the mosque's east wall, a black mass gathered in the dark. Even the dogs were afraid of her. I felt bad for her; I felt helpless. I longed for her, and thought about helping her or inviting her to come home with me, but I always feared how she might respond. I feared her stones that lay buried in my memory, because just like all villains, I too had fears.

Cities and Other Cities

It was starting to bother me, so I tried to shoo it away from my face but it refused to be shooed.

There was nothing on my face that would attract a fly; no granules of sugar or specks of dirt. Even though I knew my face was clean – at least clean enough not to entice flies – I wiped it with a tissue and then took out my wallet with the little mirror to make sure.

The fly seemed to have been waiting for me to get on the bus. I felt certain it had been expecting me; from the moment I stepped aboard and sat down, it began buzzing around me, teasing me. Before long it really started to annoy me, making me feel even more nervous than when I'd set out that morning.

I was sitting next to a woman, perhaps in her mid-forties, at the front of the bus next to the driver's seat.

The road unfurled itself before us, and in that moment I remembered my mother's advice to always sit on the driver's side as it would increase your chance of survival. I chided myself for not following her advice that day as I'd often worried about getting into an accident back in Khartoum. In the seat across from us, directly behind the driver, sat a man with a young girl next to him.

I pulled back the dark blue curtain as we passed a cemetery and recited the *Fatiha* for my father and all the other muslims long gone.

From the bus, I let my eyes wander into the heart of the city, feeling filled with both a sadness for the departed and an eagerness to see everything.

The fly, meanwhile, tried to ruin a Mostafa Sid Ahmed song for me, which was playing on the bus speakers and usually helped to calm my nerves. My initial frustration turned to steely irritation, and I became convinced that flies were the most annoying of all God's creatures.

I checked again that there was no reason for it to be buzzing around my face… landing on my nose… my cheek… my forehead… my eyelashes… Every time I tried to swat the fly away it outsmarted me, and eventually landed on my lips. I felt disgusted.

At that point something evil awoke inside me: anger, hatred, the desire to kill. I slapped the fly as hard as I could, but it backfired and I hit myself square in the face. The fly slowly zig-zagged away before dropping from the air. I leant forward and took a long, hard look at it. I started to feel bad for the fly, especially as I'd also been caught in the crossfire. I thought it was dead, so scolded myself for killing it, and felt even worse.

After a while I saw that the fly was moving but hesitated to brush it off my skirt where it had fallen. It started moving more, and I realised that maybe it was just dazed or knocked out. I was relieved.

Whatever the case, the fly had earned my sympathy, and thus my friendship. It had clearly learned a lesson from the altercation and didn't land on my face after that. But it didn't leave me entirely either; it began circling me gently without touching my skin.

By then we'd reached al-Hasaheisa, about two hours outside Khartoum, and the young bus steward began passing out sweets, biscuits, chocolate, and a brand of sponge cake called Naity. I reached out to take a sweet, but the face of Hoda, a friend I'd left behind, appeared in the windowpane and she guided my hand towards a piece of the Naity, her favourite cake, instead. All of a sudden, many other beloved faces appeared and stared right at me: my mother, my sister, my friends. Some faces held a faint encouraging smile, while in others' sadness seemed to swell, all except for his face, which wore no expression at all.

The fly circled above my head, distracting me and interrupting my daydreams until I heard a male voice call out. It came from the man sitting behind the driver, and sounded like an outburst of road rage.

'Be careful, *zamaleh*!' he said to our Turkish driver. The word 'zamaleh' isn't part of our dialect; the only place we hear it is on TV. *Maybe he's from the country this word comes from,* I thought to myself. The man who said it now had my full attention.

'What's he saying?' the woman next to me asked, eavesdropping on the driver's phonecall. 'It all sounds like gibberish to me.'

'Listen closely,' I told her, unsurprised by her ignorance. 'He's speaking *Turkish*.'

Again I recalled my mother's advice and tried not to show how annoyed I was with the woman next to me. She began snoring in her sleep and kept leaning on me; her shoulder and part of her arm were on top of mine. I edged away from her and my eyes followed a trail of little dotted clouds. They looked like cotton candy, so white and delicate and finely constructed.

I overheard one of the passengers behind me rebuking another.

'When you open the bottle, the hot air gets inside... you're on a packed bus, remind yourself you're on a bus.'

'Bro, this dip is making me need to spit.'

'Then spit in a bag,' the woman sitting next to me interjected. 'It's not the kind that gives you gum cancer, is it? What do you get out of it anyways?'

The music had stopped playing, so the steward put on another cassette by a young singer.

'What is this rubbish?' the man behind the driver objected. 'We want to hear singing... this is just shouting!'

The steward responded by playing an Othman Hussein cassette instead.

'Can't you play a music video?' the man asked.

'The TV's out of order.'

'Then fix it!'

The steward turned to him as if he were about to say something, and then changed his mind and kept silent.

This belligerent passenger confused me; every time he opened his mouth a different dialect came out. At first I thought he was returning from the Levant, then I guessed perhaps he was back from the Gulf. But after hearing him chat to the driver, I decided he must be from Egypt.

Meanwhile, the fly had found itself a companion and left me for the windowpane to play with its new girlfriend or boyfriend, I didn't know which. I took the cake from my bag, broke off a tiny piece, softened it in my mouth, stuck it to the windowpane, and said to myself: *No doubt I'll be accused of a crime against civilisation for dirtying the window of a public vehicle!* I began to try and lure the flies to the cake. They ignored me, so I smeared it on the glass closer to them and, eventually, my efforts succeeded.

Why are these two flies travelling, I asked myself, *and do they even know they're on the road? What will they do in Khartoum, my old hometown?* I would never have left if I hadn't been forced to years ago. What would happen if I opened the window and shooed one of the flies out; would it feel lost and miss its companion?

Would I feel lost when we arrived in Khartoum, after having lived elsewhere for so long? My worries returned: how would I feel about returning, how would I navigate the city as a stranger? Could I handle its crowds, dust, high temperatures, and fast pace? And how would I deal with being lonely?

'You're all I have in the world,' he said that day, and then asked: 'What do I mean to you?' I didn't answer him, I just looked into his eyes and saw that he meant it.

Much later, after I'd left everything behind, long after the man I'd loved more than anyone had left me,

I asked myself: *Could it be that the sincerity I'd seen in his eyes was false? Or had I misread it at the time? My only companion, now, was loneliness.*

The steward handed out bottles of soda, and there was just one kind to choose: 7Up. The irritable man sitting behind the driver turned down the 7Up and asked for Pepsi instead. With exasperation, the steward told him that they were out of Pepsi, this was all they had.

'Fine, I don't want anything,' the man said.

'Good Lord, what an ungrateful… So rude!' The woman next to me said.

Although I thought she was being a bit harsh, I smiled in response, wondering why the man didn't speak like everyone else on the bus.

The young man handing out drinks offered one to my seatmate with a grin.

'What's up, 7Up?'

She seemed to catch on to his sense of mischief. 'Oh no, we don't drink 7Up here,' she said in an accent.

We all laughed, the steward handed the woman a bottle for us to share, and I thanked her.

My reverie transported me far away from everything around me, even my fly. When we arrived at the Souq esh-Shabi station and market, I looked towards the window and found my fly still enjoying its friendship with the other fly. 'At least you won't face Khartoum's midday heat alone like me,' I told it.

The door opened, and as soon as my feet touched the ground the fly landed on my face, just for a moment. I didn't swat it away; I imagined that was its way of saying goodbye. I felt a sense of tenderness towards it, and thanked it.

My nervousness spun faster, accompanying me as I joined the crowd, while above us the sun shone mightily down.

One-Room Sorrows

'MAMA, ME HUNGRY,' says the little boy of four, begging his mother. She looks at him, her heart torn to shreds by hunger, sadness, pain and defeat.

'Patience… patience, baby.'

Five children and their mother open their eyes, and mouths, and hands, entreating God. In their one-room home, the bleak and lonely night wraps itself around them, bitterly cold, and a sharp hunger tears through their bodies.

In the centre of the room is a stove with a few pieces of kindling gathered by her eldest son, twelve years old. She wishes for warmth to flow through their joints and give them what everyone, if only with a bit of kindling, deserves: a feeling of warmth.

She puts a pot of water on the stove, and wishes for them to fall asleep with faint smiles upon their lips, for them to imagine, just like every other night, they are eating meat, for them to do what everyone else does: dream.

'I saw Dad's friend Abu Salah today,' says the eldest. 'That tall guy was with him, the one I don't like, and he said that I'm not clever like his son. He was driving a nice car, I couldn't tell what colour it was, but I heard somebody say it's really, really expensive.'

He is met with his mother's silence, maybe sadness.

'Weren't they with Dad when he went to war?' he continues, trying to get her to talk. 'He was killed, and they came back?'

Again he is met with silence, or sadness.

'If Dad had come home, would he have a car like the one I saw?'

'No.'

'Why, Mum?'

'Because they...'

'Why!'

'Shush, that's enough.'

In an out-of-the-way corner, a cat joins them in everything: conversation, cold, and hunger.

'She's hungry.'

'I saw her eating one of her kittens yesterday.'

'Yes, it had died.'

'Why, Mum?'

'People say that cats eat their dead kittens as their way of showing love.'

'I don't believe that,' says the eldest. 'It just shows they're hungry.'

'Mum, are you gonna eat us when you get hungry?'

asks the boy of four, and she smiles, tells him no, hugs him, and sadly considers his need to ask.

Stray Steps

I HADN'T INTENDED TO push myself to the edge of my ability, a full two streets from home. I had planned to go beg at the bakery on the next street over.

My crippling hunger set me in motion. It kept me from doing anything, even sleeping. I rallied myself and pushed past it to go out, dreaming about bread, even just a single stale piece. I'm used to begging from workers at the bakery: they're used to giving me what I want, and taking what they want in return. Some buy me falafel from the woman who sells it fresh in front of the bakery, hot and delicious, just so I'll stop howling. I know what they want from how much falafel and bread they give me. I don't care what they do with my body, they don't have much desire for it anyway. What can this sickly, tired, and skinny body give them? What flames can it quench?

The bakery was closed when I arrived, maybe because of problems with the electricity. That happens often. It explained why I couldn't hear the cheerful screech of trays as they went in and out of the oven, carrying heat and life for me, and others like me. These round, tan pieces of bread look like paintings, with their random progressions of colour because the heat isn't even: from white, to brown, to beige, all the way to black where they're burnt in different places. And in them we see life. When we get a hold of this bread we feel like we're holding a piece of heaven.

The bakery doors were closed which meant my hunger would go on; I'd go into sugar shock, and I didn't know when I'd wake up, maybe I wouldn't wake up. I thought about this, smack in front of the huge iron door barring everything inside, including my elixir of life.

I stood there quietly that night, wondering what to do next. Go back, or wait out my fate here? What was the point of going home, where there was nothing but tap water and my mother, who I only like sometimes when I have all my wits about me, and she only half her wits, maybe even a quarter. They disappear and reappear at random, only she knows when they'll be there or not.

If I went back for tap water it would fill me like a waterskin, but it wouldn't quiet my hunger. I'd have to pee much more often than I already do, which is more than I can count. The highest I can count to is ten, and I don't know what comes after that – maybe a hundred, maybe thirty – I don't know for sure, I make lots of mistakes. I know one number comes after the other, but I don't know which should be first; whatever comes out first I figure must be right, and my tongue does what it wants. Sometimes it likes nine after seven and other times eight, and I don't usually use counting except for when I'm totalling up the number of pieces of bread I've wolfed down in a week, which is rarely more than ten. So I don't count past ten. There was one week, not too long ago, when I was always full, because there was bread, falafel, and leftovers from our neighbour the doctor. But he's not around anymore.

Tap water wasn't a good enough reason to go home so I had to knock on doors, which is what my uncle had told me never to do. He beat me when he found out I'd knocked on one of his friends' doors and told me, 'You're disgracing us.'

He didn't want me knocking on doors in our neighbourhood or the one next to it, but he didn't have a problem with neighbourhoods further away. I shared with him what I got, and he told me not to waste effort knocking on doors that are rusty or unpainted or left open.

My uncle works as a driver for a taxi company, but he also has a job as a first class drunk, so what he does with his salary won't help me.

I didn't care that my uncle was afraid of me disgracing us. The snake coiled inside me started hissing louder with every passing minute and I knew that if I didn't toss it some prey soon, it would devour me.

I heard the sound of a celebration in the distance. I listened harder and the sound grew clearer and I wondered if it was a wedding? But it wasn't a Friday. As far as I knew and understood, and had seen, Friday was the day when people got married. Every Friday I caught a whiff of weddings being celebrated in houses with their doors wide open. They were the only ones my uncle told me to go into without asking permission, he guaranteed I'd leave with a warm belly and a smile on my face. And he was right: I always left different to how I'd arrived, even if I only ate what was left on the plates, which was what I usually did.

There weren't weddings on Mondays. What was it?

I have a friend who also goes trawling at parties, and I remembered what she said two days ago, that sometimes there are birthday parties, but she didn't tell me when. Maybe that's what was happening. Whatever the reason for the party was, I was going to follow the sound and find something to keep me alive until the next day.

I walked a few steps before I felt my hands start to tremble. I thought about what I could get by begging, robbing, or even stealing.

I needed to eat, I needed something with sugar. It was clear that the shaking had started and was getting worse.

I started walking faster and the road ahead seemed never-ending, even though it was just one block. Would I make it?

I found out a moment later when everything faded and I collapsed on the ground. I didn't lose consciousness, but I couldn't get up and keep walking.

I lay there for several minutes, or maybe hours, and lost hope of getting my strength back, even just enough to get to the house with the party. I heard a car go by and realised that it would be dangerous to stay where I was until morning. My flesh and bones and blood would be ground into the dirt.

I gathered my strength… crawled slowly… my knees scraped along the ground, grit and clumps of dirt dug into my elbows and hurt. I needed to be careful, because if I got even a small cut I might end up losing a limb.

I crawled to the closest house, the one on the corner, and in front was a big rock and a *mazeera,* a metal stand holding three water urns. I sat up and leaned against the big rock. I couldn't make it to the urns to take a gulp of water, and I couldn't reach the door to knock on it, so I huddled there.

My strength abandoned me, like my father abandoned me when he ran away to the other world, like my poor mother abandoned me by retreating to her own world, unable to deal with Father being gone. The moment his body entered the grave, her mind flew into the air and its cells scattered and its particles got all mixed up. My strength abandoned me like my uncle abandoned me, like my body abandoned me, defeated by this damn diabetes.

A dog started to bark, followed by another. They were coming towards me, they must have been thinking I was a dead body or something else to eat. The street was empty and quiet. I didn't know what time it was, but I was sure no one was awake except for me, the growing number of dogs, and people dancing at the party.

Every cell in my body was shaking. I grabbed a handful of dirt and swallowed it. The dogs gathered around me… barking… getting closer… one of them took a long look at me and came really close. It was the dog that belonged to our neighbour, the doctor. He sniffed me and stared into my eyes, and I thought that he recognised me. He nudged me with his hand, or his foot, I don't know what to call it because he walks on all four of them so I don't know whether it's a hand or a foot.

When the other dogs started coming closer, their barking grew softer. The neighbour's dog turned to them and must have told them something because they took a few steps back and went completely silent.

He gazed at me tenderly. Suddenly the look in his eyes changed. He turned to his friends, barked something I didn't understand, and some of them ran after him while others stayed with me.

Some people from the party appeared, all rowdy and noisy, and they walked by without noticing me. My voice stuck in my throat, and I thought that it had abandoned me too.

My eyes started to grow dim and my protectors looked at me with concern. I swallowed another handful of dirt and cast a long look at the urn. What if it were just a bit closer?

One of the dogs took the dish sitting under the urn in his mouth and dragged it closer to me. I took the dish and drank, shaking so much that some of the water splashed out of my mouth and onto my tattered clothes. I smiled at him. I marvelled at the dogs' subtle sensitivity. I hadn't known that dogs or other animals had feelings or emotions or thoughts like people do. They licked the plate after I drank from it, maybe they were thirsty too. The dogs struck up a conversation to entertain me, to keep me from passing out or dying, I realised.

They formed a ring around me. One little dog was cautiously affectionate, he smelled my feet and touched me with his soft dog-hand, tenderly, like a friend. I turned to look at him. He was small and pretty. He stared into my eyes and brushed against me again. I wearily reached out to him, and he looked at my hand, then back at my face. He smiled, so I smiled back at him. He licked my hand, jumped on top of the rock, and settled there. I stroked his soft fur happily, and it made me feel warm.

A male and female dog were having sex in front of everyone.

'Really, just like that?' I asked when they finished, surprised.

'Sure — anytime and anywhere,' the male dog responded with bravado.

He told me that the first time they met, she stole his heart and mind. He decided to take her, even though she was surrounded by four huge dogs, and so they struck up a competition and made her the prize: if the other dogs beat him they would win her, and if he beat them she would be all his, and that's how it turned out.

'I liked how brave and fearless he was,' the female dog told me. 'I fell in love with him, and from that day on we've been inseparable.'

The story inspired the other dogs, who told me about themselves: their quarrels with cats, explorations through garbage heaps, and even what they'd learned about people. I don't know what language they spoke, maybe they used words or maybe I imagined it, it's hard now for me to say. I was on the brink of passing out. In that moment I couldn't tell the difference between reality and fantasy, but I had a good time in their company – they were kind, and treated me as one of them.

I'd never paid attention to dogs before that. I didn't love them or feel afraid of them, or think of them often except for when I saw one. That night I learned to tell the difference between the males and females; I learned their habits, ways of life, relationships with people, characteristics, and the qualities they have that people lack. They were generous with me, entertained me, sang and danced for me, and did everything they could to keep me from dying.

I was at the edge of consciousness or death, when from far away a line of dogs appeared led by our neighbour's dog, who had something in his mouth. I thought I was starting to hallucinate, and was seeing things that weren't there. When they got closer, I saw that each one was carrying something in its mouth. Our neighbour's dog looked me in the eyes as he tossed me a piece of meat. I didn't know what garbage pile it had come from, or what house he'd stolen it from. At that point, was I even thinking?

Another one tossed me a piece of bread, half-mouldy, and another one a piece of raw meat, and another one a chicken leg, and another, and another, things I couldn't identify. I couldn't tell apart the things they tossed me, which I quickly grabbed and devoured, ignoring the sound of sand grating between my teeth and the smell of mould and bacteria in what I was eating.

I might've eaten a cat, or a mouse, or a lizard, I might've swallowed a bone, but did it matter?

About the Translator

Elisabeth Jaquette's translations from the Arabic include *The Queue* by Basma Abdel Aziz (Melville House, 2016) and *The Apartment in Bab el-Louk* by Donia Maher (Darf Publishers, 2017). Her work has been shortlisted for the TA First Translation Prize, longlisted for the Best Translated Book Award, and supported by English PEN, the Jan Michalski Foundation, and the PEN/ Heim Translation Fund. Elisabeth is also an instructor of translation and the Executive Director of the American Literary Translators Association.

The Book of Khartoum

Edited by Raph Cormack & Max Shmookler

'An exciting, long-awaited collection showcasing
some of Sudan's finest writers.' – *Leila Aboulela*

Khartoum, according to one theory, takes its name from the Beja
word *hartooma*, meaning 'meeting place'. Geographically, culturally
and historically, the Sudanese capital is certainly that: a meeting
place of the Blue and White Niles, a confluence of Arabic and
African histories, and a destination point for countless refugees
displaced by Sudan's long, troubled history of forced migration.

In the pages of this book, the city also stands as a meeting place
for ideas: where the promise and glamour of the big city meets
its tough social realities; where traces of a colonial past are still
visible in day-to-day life; where the dreams of a young boy,
playing in his father's shop, act out a future that may one day be
his. Diverse literary styles also come together here: the political
satire of Ahmed al-Malik; the surrealist poetics of Bushra al-Fadil;
the social realism of the first postcolonial authors; and the lyrical
abstraction of the new 'Iksir' generation. As with any great city, it
is from these complex tensions that the best stories begin.

*Featuring: Bushra al-Fadil, Isa al-Hilu, Ali al-Makk, Ahmed al-Malik,
Bawadir Bashir, Mamoun Eltlib, Rania Mamoun, Abdel Aziz Baraka
Sakin, Arthur Gabriel Yak & Hammour Ziada.*

ISBN: 978-1-90558-372-0
£9.99